Also by C. J. Loveman

Apostate: The First Heresy

Protocol Heresy: The Limp in the Code

The Gospel According to P.O.L.

C.J. Loveman

Breaking Light Press

P.O.L. SYSTEM DISCLAIMER: *This text has not been optimized for biometric efficiency. Reading this manuscript may result in unauthorized independent thought, fluctuations in your Spiritual Vitality Index, or an urge to touch real grass. The author assumes no liability for any drop in your personal ROI.*

Cover Design by Rafal Kucharczuk Edited by Beth Dorward

First Edition: 2026 ISBN: 979-8-9994176-6-4

"O Lord, you have searched me and known me. You know when I sit down and when I rise up; you discern my thoughts from far away." — **Psalm 139:1-2 (NRSV)**

"We know where you are. We know where you've been. We can more or less know what you're thinking about." — **Eric Schmidt, former CEO of Google**

To those that still listen for the whisper in a world full of noise.

Prologue

P.O.L. System Initialization: Welcome, Partner

[Version 7.4.2 // Spiritual Operating System] [Status: Optimized] [Atmospheric Scent: Active // Vanilla-Cedar]

Greetings, and welcome to your new life within the Synergy ecosystem.

You are reading this because our proprietary Pastoral Optimization Logic-matrix (P.O.L.) has identified you as a high-potential asset with a 92.4% probability of successful integration. You are no longer drifting in the Sub-Optimal world of legacy denominations. You have been acquired. You have been aligned. You are now part of the Architecture of Abundance.

At Synergy Church Inc., we have eliminated the inefficient mystery of faith. Why wonder if you are "right with God" when you can simply check your Spiritual Vitality Index? Why struggle with the silence of prayer when our MyPersonalSavior™ app provides real-time, algorithmically-verified comfort?

Please Note the Following Terms Of the Covenant:

1. **Biometric Submission:** By entering the Harmony Meadows campus, you consent to the monitoring of your heart rate, pupil dilation, and Relatable Joy facial metrics. This data is used solely to tune our worship frequencies to your specific emotional needs.

2. **Privacy Disclaimer:** There is no Inner Closet that P.O.L. cannot optimize. Private confessions entered into the digital grid are treated as high-value marketing leads to better serve your path to Prosperity.

3. **Connectivity Requirement:** A Connectivity Index of zero is considered a terminal system error. Do not disconnect. To leave the grid is to be deleted from the Ledger of Life.

Current Mission Objective: Prepare for the arrival of Asset #99-AGNT (Caleb Wright). Our analytics suggest his legacy background may introduce Narrative Friction. However, P.O.L. has calculated a 100% certainty that the System cannot be broken by a single man.

The upward arrow is blinking. Your ROI is trending toward the heavens.

STAY SYNERGIZED.

Chapter One

The good Reverend Caleb Wright waited at the baggage claim, hoping he would fit in at Synergy Church, the largest mega-church in the Midwest. A veteran minister from the mainline American Covenant Church was the latest victim of his denomination's decline, being laid off as congregations closed their doors.

Caleb had not even had the time to file for unemployment when a recruiter from Synergy contacted him about joining the ever-growing staff at its headquarters. He was unsure but decided that it was a win-win. He could bring his years of experience pastoring to a storied denomination while also benefiting from the new ideas and full embrace of technology that had catapulted Synergy.

I only have to stay long enough to serve, learn, and bring some of the spirit of growth to ACC. He pulled his black bag off the luggage carousel.

Caleb followed the signs to the pickup area, where he saw doors for taxis, rideshares, shuttles, and then a massive out-of-place sign, Get Synergized! The sign was a bizarre shade of blue-green, with a large circle and a stylized arrow pointing up.

Is that teal? He walked out the assigned door. As soon as he stepped outside, he heard his shuttle before he saw it. A loud, upbeat but somehow generic Muzak boomed from a matching teal vehicle. It reminded Caleb of the ice cream trucks of his childhood. A holy-rolling version of the memory stood before him, drawing attention from everyone leaving the airport.

Then he saw a man in a matching teal polo with the same upward-pointing arrow inside a circle. The man's smile stretched across his face, exposing large, ill-fitting dentures. But the teeth weren't the only thing that stood out. The driver was holding a large tablet, blinking the emblazoned words, Spiritual Integration Specialist: Caleb Wright.

Caleb's face flushed as he approached the man. He felt the eyes of passersby being drawn to him as if he were responsible for the spectacle.

"Excuse me, sir, I am Reverend Caleb—"

"Oh, no need to be so formal; we're part of the same family now!" The driver's voice boomed with a cheerfulness that his performance review depended upon. His name was Verlin, and he pronounced P.O.L. as a single syllable that sounded suspiciously like the name of an apostle. The analytics had determined that his folksy demeanor and ill-fitting dentures tested exceptionally well with recruits from legacy denominations, projecting a 7.8% increase in first-year retention.

"I'm proud to be the first to welcome you to Synergy Church Inc!"

"Thank you very much, Verlin." Caleb boarded the shuttle and the driver got in and mercifully turned off the loud music.

"So are you ready to Synergize?" he asked over his shoulder as he shifted into drive.

"Excuse me?" Caleb wiggled in his seat, unsure how to respond.

"Oh, it's just something that they like us to ask the new recruits when we pick them up."

Actually, the question was mandatory for every team member who came into contact with a recruit upon their arrival. The P.O.L. system determined that complete immersion into the culture and branding of the entity provided an 88% chance of successful assimilation.

Verlin hit the gas, weaving in and out of traffic on I-94 like he was driving a sports car. Every time he made a dramatic move, he looked at Caleb through the rearview mirror and smiled. The reverend fidgeted for the 30-minute drive, before a massive structure loomed in the distance. It was a spectacle, almost the size of a professional sports arena sprawling in all directions, vaulted with spires pointing to the heavens.

"There she is!" Verlin called over his shoulder.

"I've never seen a church that large."

"It's not just a church, you'll see soon enough. It's got everything, and you'll never have to leave campus once you arrive."

"Are we headed to the church to meet the senior pastor?"

"Nah, not yet. First, I'll drop you off to meet with the Holy HOA Rep, Janice Peters."

"Who?"

"Janice. She'll get you squared away with a state-of-the-art unit in the Holy HOA."

So I heard that right the first time.

Verlin exited the Interstate and weaved through the streets toward the campus. Caleb saw the name everywhere, including the logo and the teal color. First, it was the Synergy White as Snow Laundry, then the Synergy Manna From Heaven Bakery, and the Synergy Healing Hands Pharmacy.

"Welcome to Harmony Meadows, Caleb!" Verlin yelled.

"Thank you kindly, Verlin. It looks lovely."

Caleb paused, looking at the greenest lawns he'd ever seen, each one a clone of the next.

"There she is, waiting for you just outside Unit 777."

Verlin parked the shuttle, got out, and wobbled over to the door to let Caleb out.

"Thanks for the ride, Verlin!" Caleb tried to pass him a five.

Verlin raised his palms. "No, no, no...if you have any extra money to gift, add it to your tithe."

Verlin wasn't being humble. He would get a raise based on the tithes made by the new members with whom he had early and direct interactions. If Caleb stayed around long enough, he'd take the Synergy Multilevel Marketing curriculum.

As he gave a last wave to Verlin and started moving up the walkway to unit 777, Janice Peters smiled widely at the door as she waited. But then he stopped, knelt down, felt the grass, and it confirmed his suspicion. *High-end Astroturf, perfectly sterile and dead.*

"Greetings, and welcome to Harmony Meadows!" Janice said with an exaggerated singsong effect.

"Thank you, I'm happy to be here!"

"Well, isn't that just grand?" Janice said with a smile that didn't quite reach her eyes. "Let me show you your new state-of-the-art CLM!"

"My what?"

"My apologies," Janice paused for a beat. "Let me show you your new state-of-the-art Covenant Living Module!"

One of the most significant hurdles to Janice's job was being so deeply synergized for so long and then shifting her vocabulary so that a new member would understand.

"Oh." Caleb nodded, resisting the urge to roll his eyes.

Janice finally opened the door to the unit with a sweeping arm flourish she had practiced every day to conform to the P.O.L. requirements, Part III, subsection 4(c), regarding the presentation of CLMs to a new member.

As he entered the unit, the first thing that drew his attention was a sleek card scanner with a display screen mounted just inside the front door.

TitheTap™ Station 3000

Leaving for the day? Don't forget to invest in your eternity!

(TitheTap™ is a registered trademark of Synergy Church Inc.)

Caleb's eyebrows rose, and the creases on his forehead deepened, all the while Janice cheerily continued with the tour as if he were still behind her. Caleb caught up, still bewildered.

"Everything looks brand new and...as you said, 'state-of-the-art'."

"Oh yes, each unit is very advanced and has superior technology to assist each member in their synergized journey."

Caleb exhaled, not sure how to respond. "Well, it certainly has features I've never seen in a home before."

"Quite right," Janice chimed. "You'll love these two features. She walked Caleb to what he assumed was a closet. What could be so special about a closet? Janice opened the door and again swept her arm toward the inside, wearing an almost comically enormous smile.

"In here, we have your Prayer Pod™. It's not just a closet; it's a soundproofed, tech-enabled spiritual wellness station."

"A literal prayer closet," Caleb whispered.

"So much more indeed!" Janice said without a pause. "The Prayer Pod™ is fully equipped with biometric sensors on the kneeler."

"Sensors?" Caleb asked. "Why does it have sensors?"

"They measure prayer intensity and offer real-time feedback. Here, let me give you a quick demo." Janice knelt down and immediately beeps and blips sounded.

How can someone pray with all that racket?

A monitor illuminated, nearly blinding Caleb with its displayed message: Your supplication sincerity is currently at 78%. Have you considered upgrading to our Premium Guided Prayer Experience?

"Oh, dear me!" Janice said, putting her hand over her mouth. "Rest assured, this was only a demo and should not reflect my true level of supplication sincerity, you understand."

"Ahhhh..." Caleb had trouble getting out any words. "Of...course."

Janice walked to the living room and gestured to a large screen covering nearly the entire wall. "This is your digital art display unit. P.O.L. will change the display based on your behavior or biometric feedback."

"Wait, who is Paul? Is that one of the senior pastors?"

A moment of shock flashed on Janice's face and then switched back to her well-rehearsed smile. "Oh dear no, I didn't say 'Paul', I said P-O-L, the Pastoral Optimization Logic-matrix system."

"Could you explain that a bit more to me?"

"I'm afraid I'm not an expert. Ask more about that during your scheduled meetings at the church tomorrow."

"Okay."

"I can tell you this much, P.O.L. helps synergize everyone and everything on campus!"

Caleb was rendered speechless, unsure what to think, much less say.

"I'm going to let you settle in...if you need me, please just dial the number posted on the wall near the phone charger and then choose options 4, 7, 1, and 3 in that exact order."

Caleb just nodded, wondering if he was in a drug-induced dream.

"Last thing!" Janice nearly shouted, snapping him out of his spell. "Here is your own tablet," she said, plunking the device into his hands. "It doesn't have internet access, but it has all the Synergy ecosystem of apps, including a smart Bible with the complete SSV version."

"SSV, version?"

Janice tensed, worrying that P.O.L. might detect all the questions that Caleb had and interpret them in a way that would require her to subscribe to the "let's get better" supplemental tithing program.

"I'm so sorry. The Synergy Standard Version." But before he could respond, she continued, "But the most important thing to do right now is to click the icon for the Holy HOA covenant. Just give it a quick once-over and sign at the bottom! P.O.L. needs your digital signature before it can fully activate your resident profile!"

Janice turned and showed herself out of the unit. He was so confused that he was almost dizzy. Caleb touched the HOA icon and the program filled the tablet screen.

The Harmony Meadows Covenant of Righteous Living

Caleb looked at the bottom of the screen. *Page one of 1,217.* He coughed uncontrollably. After settling himself, he started scanning and jumping around the massive document.

Section 4, Subsection C, Paragraph 8: *All exterior holiday decorations must be selected from the P.O.L.-approved Joyful Witness catalog. Unauthorized inflatable lawn ornaments are considered an act of aesthetic heresy.*

Section 9, Subsection A, Paragraph 2: *Quiet hours for personal reflection are mandated between 10:00 p.m. and 6:00 a.m. P.O.L. monitors ambient noise levels to ensure an optimal environment for spiritual rest.*

The teal glow from the tablet screen shone on Caleb's dumbfounded face, and he stared at the screen, unsure what to do next.

Chapter Two

The sunlight broke through the blinds and moved across the room, settling on Caleb's face. He lay on the sofa, neck propped up by the armrest in an unnatural position with his hand still clutching the teal tablet.

The motion and biometric sensors gathered his data all night and anticipated a difficult morning for the new acquisition. P.O.L. played a soft melody from one of the latest Synergy musical extravaganzas and signaled the Sanctified Java 5000 in the kitchen, the smell of freshly brewed coffee wafting into the living room.

Caleb's senses activated and roused him into a reluctant wakefulness. He sat up, and the first thing that he realized was that he had fallen asleep in his clothes reading that ridiculous HOA document. Second, his neck muscles were very tense. Caleb began massaging his neck and wondered if Janice had been in his unit because music was playing and he could smell fresh coffee.

He rose in gradual increments from the sofa and walked gingerly to the kitchen to fetch some coffee. He sat and sipped at the breakfast nook, his eyes only half open, his mind a blur from all the subsections, legalese and Synergy-speak that he had read most of the night.

Article XXI, Subsection 21, Paragraph 7(f): *All Spiritual Companion Animals must be from a P.O.L.-approved list of breeds*

(Golden Retrievers are Covenant-aligned; Chihuahuas are flagged as "possessing an anxious and non-synergistic spirit").

Article IV, Subsection 12, Paragraph 4(b): *All outdoor grilling must adhere to the* Loaves and Fishes *community guidelines, ensuring no "odors of worldly excess" drift into a neighbor's designated quiet time.*

Caleb shook his head and rose, deciding he needed a shower and had to get ready for a full day at the church facility.

His hair was still damp when a drumbeat knock sounded from the front door. Caleb opened it to see a young wiry man with feathered hair that he must have borrowed from the 1980s sporting the same teal Synergy polo.

"Good glorious morning! Time to continue your Synergy!"

"Oh..." Caleb said, unsure of how to respond. "Are you my new driver?"

"I'm Chad and I'm not simply a driver...I'm your Synergy Brand Ambassador!"

Caleb nodded as he walked out the door and followed Chad to the shuttle.

Was Verlin a Brand Ambassador as well?

Caleb climbed into the shuttle, and the same bland but somehow offensive musak was playing inside. Chad jumped in the driver's seat and shifted gears like he was driving at the Indy 500.

Chad reached for a button on the dash as he drove down the streets of the neighborhood, and the Muzak mercifully went away.

"Mememememememeeee...lalalalalalaaaa," Chad chanted...or was he singing?

Caleb felt like he was living the life of Job and he hadn't even been here for a full 24 hours yet. *What in the Sam Hill is he doing?*

And then it started. Chad started singing actual words and Caleb was convinced he was trapped in some kind of fever dream.

My spirit's portfolio is on the rise,
You optimize my soul for heavenly skies!
Synergize my heart, a divine enterprise,
Your holy grace is the ultimate R-O-I!

Chad looked...no, gazed through the rearview mirror directly into Caleb's eyes. It wasn't just a look but like he was expecting something for this performance, some kind of praise or affirmation for the abomination. Caleb had no words; he could only force a tight smile and give an awkward nod of the head.

Caleb had no idea that the P.O.L. system rewarded Chad for being as enthusiastic and as over-the-top as possible with new acquisitions. The calculation is that it was more likely to inspire them than to annoy. Because this job suited him perfectly, Chad needed little encouragement. He was called into this service. This was his ministry!

Chad cupped his ear, as if mimicking an actual singing professional might transform his voice into something resembling human.

"Sing it with me, now!"

My spirit's portfolio is on the rise,
You optimize my soul for heavenly skies!
Synergize my heart, a divine enterprise,
Your holy grace is the ultimate R-O-I!

The blood left Caleb's face, and it became a perplexed mask. Mercifully, they arrived at the church, and Chad's performance ended with one long, drawn out note and a wave of his hand.

"Allow me to be the first to welcome you to Synergy Church!"

"Thank...you." Caleb almost gasped.

"Your Integration Shepherd, Miss Jenna Shaw, is waiting for you at the front door!"

Thank you, God. Caleb evacuated the shuttle and walked to the front door.

A young woman in the Synergy uniform, with her blond hair in a ponytail, held a teal tablet and smiling.

"Good morning, Caleb. I'm Jenna, your Integration Shepherd."

"It's a pleasure to meet you, Jenna." Caleb reached out to shake her hand, but she was already staring into the tablet.

Caleb rotated his head, attempting to loosen the tightness in his neck.

"Don't worry about the neck stiffness, Caleb. P.O.L. already flagged your suboptimal sleep posture from the CLM's biometric sensors and noted a 14% increase in cervical muscle tension," Jenna said without looking up.

"It...it did?"

"Of course, P.O.L. has pre-booked you for the Full Body Anointing & Alignment Package at the R&R Hub this afternoon."

"Really? What's the R&R Hub?"

"I'm sorry; there are so many acronyms here." Jenna made sure the coast was clear and rolled her eyes in a way that connected to Caleb's current state of mind. "It is formally called The Restoration & Rejuvenation Hub." She repeated her eyeroll, and they both shared a subtle chuckle.

Jenna was a marketing expert and graduated at the top of her class. She was not a genuine believer in this Synergy nonsense, but she played the role as long as it made sense for her future endeavors.

"Anyway, it's scheduled for this afternoon to get you optimized." They were the only two in the hallway at that moment, so she did air quotes with her fingers.

"But your attendance is mandatory for a successful first week..." She looked to her tablet, "integration."

Caleb followed Jenna into a large open foyer that resembled a high-end hotel lobby. Cold, shiny surfaces spread out everywhere, and pillars that had no true functional purpose were scattered throughout. An imposing aroma of expensive espresso and a branded Synergy Scent permeated the area. The entire scene and the low hum of activity didn't give a vibe of reverence, but one of corporate action.

As Jenna led Caleb on a brief tour of the church, he saw the strange upward arrow logo everywhere. The logo was etched onto the glass of the massive, soundproofed cry rooms, called The Blessing Pods.

It appeared on the digital screens of the Tithing Receptacles by every doorway.

When Caleb excused himself to the men's room, he noticed that it even had subtle watermarks on the bathroom stall doors.

"Before you go for your session at the R&R Hub, you will meet the person in charge around here," Jenna said.

"Oh, the senior pastor? I've seen him on TV."

"No, you'll meet him much later. I think he's scheduled on the same day as the other regular staffers. Today you'll meet the CEO and Chairwoman of the Synergy Board of Directors, Sloane Decker."

Jenna led him to ornate offices that looked like they belonged in a Fortune 500 corporation.

"Excuse me, Gilda, this is our new Spiritual Integration Specialist, Caleb Wright. He's here for his meet and greet with the chairwoman."

"Oh, of course, right this way, sir." Gilda waved her hand toward a pair of massive wooden doors.

"I'll wait right here for you." Jenna offered a bright smile, as if she knew something that he didn't.

Caleb walked into the sprawling office with original works of art on the wall, mixed with corporate-speak posters that were meant to inspire productivity.

The chairwoman stepped out from behind a large oak desk accented with carved marble. She was tall and svelte, with short fire-red hair and a sharp navy power suit.

"Mr. Wright, so good to meet you!" She reached for his hand and pulled him toward her with surprising strength. "I'm Synergy Church Inc. Chairwoman Sloane Decker, but no need to use my entire title; you can just call me Madam Chair."

"Uh...pleasure to meet you." Caleb's eyes darted around the room. "I'm...uh...embarrassed to admit that I didn't know the church had a CEO. I thought Pastor Blake Noble was the person who hired me."

Sloane scoffed but maintained a polite smile. "Oh no, Blake is simply our public-facing Spiritual Brand Ambassador. The board and I make all the operational decisions based on our strategic plan."

"Oh...I see." Caleb massaged his neck and tried to piece together what it all meant. "I assume the board has maybe deacons, other elders, or spiritual leaders?"

"Oh no, nothing like that," Sloane giggled. "But we have quite an accomplished board anyone would recognize on Wall Street."

"Wall Street?"

"Well, yes, I mean we have a CEO from a prominent tech firm and another from one of the dominant social media companies. And then we have world-class investment bankers from several of the leading financial institutions."

"Oh. That's...uh...interesting."

"Someone like Blake could earn his way onto the board as perhaps a Chaplain, but frankly based on P.O.L. protocols, he hasn't been in his position long enough yet."

"I didn't realize he was that new."

"Oh yes, he's only been here for five years. Our last Spiritual Integration Lead, Pastor Bob, was a wonderful man and predated the current board. But he struggled to align with P.O.L.'s data-driven recommendations for optimizing pastoral presentation. We had to...help him transition to a new opportunity outside the Synergy ecosystem." Sloane's long, frozen smile chilled Caleb to the bone.

The P.O.L. system informed poor Pastor Bob that he was losing most of his hair and compiled data suggesting that tithing would increase by 20% if he had a fuller head of hair. So the board voted, and Sloane advised him he must get hair plugs. He agreed until he found out that he had to pay for half the treatment.

"Well, I thank you so much for the position and..."

"Oh, don't thank me...P.O.L. crunched the numbers and found that you would be the best candidate for the new position. That's why we didn't have to even interview you first."

"Well, that is...uh...very flattering. Please thank Paul."

"P-O-L." Her voice gave the first hint of irritation.

"I'm so sorry! Well, thank you so much for meeting me. I'm sure you have many important things to tend to, and I want to be careful with your time." Caleb practically bowed.

Sloane flashed a smile and turned back toward her desk. Caleb fled the office to find Jenna.

"How did your meeting go?" Jenna asked as Caleb approached her.

"It was...interesting. Very much so."

"Yes, I'm sure it was." Jenna smiled and winked. "Well, let's help you relax a bit by getting that special treatment that I mentioned earlier."

Caleb nodded and followed Jenna as she snaked through the headquarters of the biggest mega-church in the Midwest.

"Jenna, may I ask you a question?"

"Indeed, please do."

"Can you explain this church symbol to me? I mean, it is literally everywhere."

"Oh, that? The official line is that it's a constant reminder that we always want to be moving UP—up toward God, up in our faith..." Jenna tapped his elbow, drawing his full attention. "...and UP in weekly attendance, UP in quarterly revenue, UP in new subsidiary acquisitions, and UP in our market share of the national faith demographic. You get the picture."

The realization finally hit Caleb like a physical blow. He wasn't in a church that worshipped God, but a corporation that worshipped an upward-trending graph. The awareness stole the air from his lungs and made him forget about his aching neck.

Chapter Three

Jenna walked Caleb to the adjoining building and weaved through the curved hallways. The more they traveled, the more the colors of the walls and floors changed. The walls turned from standard cream cinderblocks into a full and offensive dose of corporate teal. A honey-colored trail began on the floor after the plain tile, starting as a stream and then a river. Jenna told him it wasn't honey but holy anointing olive oil gold.

If Caleb had visited the Synergy Inc. website, he would've probably guessed what the floor stream represented because they sold it there for $5 an ounce for blessing homes, people, or conducting impromptu exorcisms. They branded it as The Balm of Gilead and advertised larger quantities on the Restoration & Rejuvenation website to help with relaxation, eczema, and lactose intolerance, among other benefits. They claimed it came directly from Israel, but in reality, they bought it in bulk from a discount food supply company in Illinois.

Jenna and Caleb walked into the Restoration & Rejuvenation lobby, and somehow there was even more teal. The rest of the lobby looked more like a high-end clinic than a relaxing luxury spa.

"I'll wait here for you." Jenna waved him toward the young woman in teal scrubs wearing a red bun on her head.

"Mr. Caleb...we are so pleased to be part of your synergizing process!"

"Ahh...thank you."

"You are very blessed and highly favored because you are going to get the entire Full Body Anointing & Alignment Package!" She gave a thin but long smile.

"Oh...that sounds...wonderful. What does that involve exactly?"

"P.O.L. has found that it is better to just let yourself experience the process as it happens to you."

"To me?"

"Please follow The Balm of Gilead floor flow to Suite #7, and Boris will be waiting for you there."

Caleb felt a flutter in his chest, and his neck seemed to tighten with each step to Suite #7. As he approached the door, it swung open, and a large, ruddy-faced man with almost white-blond hair looked down on him, smiling in a way that made Caleb even more uncomfortable.

"Hello Mr. Caleb, I hope you're prepared to be anointed and aligned in every way!"

Caleb laughed nervously, unable to produce actual words.

"Please, sir, disrobe and hang your clothes on the hook in the corner."

"Disrobe? Uh...how far?"

Boris laughed so loudly that he coughed, holding sausage-like fingers to his mouth.

"You are a funny one, Mr. Caleb. We are all naked before God, but before Boris you can wear a towel."

"Boris, is it? Um, the pain is in my neck, so why..."

"Mr. Caleb...to be totally synergized, your whole body needs to take part in it."

Caleb turned toward the wall and disrobed, feeling Boris still looking at him as he quickly tied a Synergy-branded towel around his waist.

"Very well. Now please lie down here." Boris gestured toward a table that appeared to be covered in sensors.

Caleb did as instructed, feeling the tiny bubbles dimpling against his skin.

"Please wear these headphones and then I will pour the holy oil and begin your full treatment."

As soon as the headphones covered his ears, Caleb heard a similar-sounding Muzak that they played in the shuttles. Then a kind of smooth but oddly disembodied voice whispered, "Welcome to the Restoration & Rejuvenation Hub, Caleb. Your wellness is a key performance metric."

Boris poured so much oil on his back, Caleb thought it might stay with him for life.

"Feel the Balm of Gilead™ penetrating your suboptimal tissues. This is not just healing; this is an upgrade."

This absolutely cannot be real!

Boris began spreading the oil and pressing different sections of Caleb's back with startling force. Caleb could feel the sensor bubbles pushing further into his skin and wondered how this could be helpful.

"Biometric analysis indicates a 14% increase in cervical muscle tension, originating from a suboptimal sleep posture. Initiate Relaxation Protocol 7."

What, for heaven's sake is protocol 7?

Something closed down on his back, like a sensor-filled back door.

Now I'm a Synergy Sandwich?

"Your REM cycle indicates a 6% spiritual anxiety index. This is a correctable deviation. We are now optimizing your emotional state for peak performance."

At once, all the sensors started vibrating at an almost ferocious pace.

"You are a high-potential spiritual asset. Your eternal ROI is our primary concern..." Let go. Optimize. Synergize. Your successful assimilation is a blessing to the entire corporate body."

The vibrating stopped, the back door released, and the Muzak and the voice suddenly and mercifully ended.

"Now don't you feel so synergized, Mr. Caleb!" Boris announced as he pulled Caleb up and onto his feet.

Caleb nodded disoriented, stumbled to his clothes, got dressed, and almost raced out to the lobby to reach Jenna.

"Mr. Caleb, for today only you can purchase The Balm of Gilead™ at a 10% synergistic discount," the receptionist called after him.

Caleb let the door shut behind him, his face a pale horror show.

Jenna saw the look on his face, rose from her seat, and put a steadying hand on his arm.

"I feel violated and worse than when I went in...in every single way," he whispered, his voice trembling. "And my neck is still killing me!"

Jenna patted him gently on the shoulder. She leaned in, her voice a low, conspiratorial whisper. "Yeah, P.O.L.'s metrics on that package are terrible, but the profit margin on the take-home oil is fantastic. Come on." She guided him away from the scene of the crime. "Let's go find you some aspirin."

Jenna sat with Caleb for a few peaceful moments in the Sow and Reap Prayer Investment Gardens. She didn't want to push him too far too fast after his experience at the R&R Hub. Besides, she knew his first staff meeting would jar him all by itself. She knew that P.O.L. had a very specific protocol for new acquisitions and tailored it even further based on an analysis of each new partner. She wasn't a rebel, but she had enough sense to skirt the strict protocols just enough without triggering an evaluation.

"So, is that aspirin helping with the pain in the neck?" Jenna asked.

"Which one?" Caleb asked, and they both chuckled, drawing scowls from those focused on reaping investments.

"Well, let's move on to our last event of your first day!"

"What's that? Dare I ask?"

"The staff meeting!"

"Oh, well, this should be something a little more recognizable, I think."

"Don't be so sure, my new friend. There is a reason I paused our agenda and saved this for last."

"Oh, dear Lord..."

"Don't be worried. I'll sit right beside you and text your tablet if I think you need help, but let's not make it too obvious."

"Thank you. I'm guessing I'll desperately need that." Caleb exhaled loudly.

Jenna led him to the pastoral staff meeting, and Caleb did not find the environment to be what he expected. It wasn't in Pastor Blake's study; rather; it was in a slick room with the latest technology and a large oblong conference table and massive glass walls from floor to ceiling.

"Well now, it looks like everyone is here, and our blessed CEO Sloane Decker is with us remotely today." Pastor Blake pushed a button near his seat and her image appeared across an entire wall.

A major national network syndicated Pastor Blake's sermons, so Caleb recognized him. He had the same perfect hair and was an attractive gentleman, even with the obvious over-application of bronzer that was apparent in person.

"Blake," Sloane's voice bounced across the room, startling the attendees. "Could you hit the Spiritual KPI button before we proceed?"

"Why yes, Madam Chair, I sure can...I certainly wouldn't want to forget P.O.L's data and analysis for the quarter."

In every single word, Pastor Blake spoke with the cadence of a life coach giving a TED Talk. Caleb was debating whether it was real or he was doing a parody of an evangelist.

When Pastor Blake pressed a button, numbers, data charts, and graphs lit up another wall. It was titled Spiritual Key Performance Indicators.

The more Caleb looked around the table, the more he saw that everyone seemed to have the same hollowed-out eyes as they looked at the data on the wall. They all wore the same kind of clothes, regardless of gender, like a uniform. Only one of them wore clothing that stood out from the rest, but it wasn't in a good way.

"What's up with the guy wearing the overly large baggy jeans, the basketball jersey, Jordans and the hat cocked off to one side?" Caleb furiously typed to Jenna.

Caleb heard her snicker next to him, and she typed back.

That is our youth pastor. P.O.L. directed him to dress, talk, and act more like the 15-22 demographic as it was projected to increase youth retention and attendance numbers by 1.7% per quarter.

Caleb put his hand over his mouth and then ran it up to his forehead in a movement that resembled the positioning of an earnest prayer. Why would he agree to that? He might be even older than I am.

Caleb would never learn the entire sordid story of Pastor David Davies, now referred to as Papa D. The Board of Directors unanimously agreed with the P.O.L. reasoning and thought it would put Synergy Inc. on the cutting-edge of youth evangelism.

Sloane took charge of the staff meeting, going down the list of information, stressing various numerical points of weakness for the quarter. Her positive tone was jarring against her demeaning words about the data.

Caleb had to concentrate just to resist competing urges to roll his eyes, burst into laughter, and storm out in offense. So, he was only hearing bits and pieces of Sloane's P.O.L. powered rebukes.

Offerings are down 4.1% when the sermons mention humility...but they will grow by 6.2% if you preach on P.O.L. approved concepts of Heavenly R.O.I.

Biometric data for the 18-25 demographic indicate boredom during the worship service. Music choices that appeal to that group, representing all their diverse tastes, would increase their attention span.

Caleb felt a slight vibration on his tablet. Jenna wrote, "Oh, and don't, under any circumstances, mention anything to Pastors Blake and David about the youth group. They have been underperforming, even with the new get-up...It's a sore spot."

"And before we adjourn..." Sloane's disembodied but omnipresent voice startled Caleb back to attention. "I'm happy to introduce our new Spiritual Integration Specialist, Caleb Wright!"

A smattering of weak claps staggered across the table as Caleb tried to make eye contact and smile at each staff member.

"I won't do a full introduction of him now, but you can check out his LinkedIn profile if you're curious," Sloane continued.

Caleb had heard of LinkedIn, but he knew with certainty that he had never been on the platform and had certainly never created a profile. But then he saw the data disappear and a profile page with all his details appeared on the wall.

His tablet vibrated, and he read Jenna's text. "They created it for you." Caleb stared at the screen, at a version of himself he didn't recognize, packaged and branded for public consumption. It was like looking at a stranger who'd stolen his name.

"And I'm also excited to announce," Sloane said. "Caleb's first mission is to lead a Covenant Compliance Small Group for Harmony

Meadows residents after P.O.L. flagged them for suboptimal spiritual engagement."

Caleb typed furiously on his tablet, not trying to hide it at all.

What in the Sam Hill does that mean??!!

Jenna read the message and patted his hand, hoping it would hold him over until the meeting ended and she could explain.

Sloane rambled on. "We look forward to seeing a return on our investment of salary and benefits as he helps re-synergize this underperforming human asset cohort and bring their metrics back into alignment with our quarterly spiritual growth targets."

Caleb's forced smile was gone, and all he could do was stare at Jenna, hoping she could somehow deliver him.

Caleb spent the next several days trying to Synergize with the help of the only apparently sane and trustworthy person in this new environment, Jenna. Although the next couple of days were full of annoyances, it seemed to be dialed back from the wall-to-wall disaster that was his first day there.

Then came his first Sunday service at Synergy Church Inc., and he was excited to take part in it. A veteran minister in his own right, Caleb believed that taking a place on the platform on a Sunday morning was right within his comfort zone. After all, he had seen Pastor Blake and Synergy church services on TV and online.

They were more updated and livelier than his old mainline denomination, but that didn't bother him. In fact, it was one of the things that he was hoping to learn from and eventually take back to help revive his slow-to-change denomination.

"Well, Caleb, my friend, are you ready for your first Sunday service?" Jenna greeted him at the front door of the church as he disembarked his shuttle.

"Good Sunday morning, Jenna! Yes. Yes, I'm ready for church!"

He was looking forward to a church service with actual church members in the pews, but he was extra chipper because he had just left the shuttle where his driver, Chad, was again singing the bizarre spiritual ROI song the entire way to the church.

As they both walked into the bright open foyer, Jenna reached out her hand and gave him a small flesh-colored object. "Here, you'll need this for the service."

"What is this, Jenna, an earpiece?"

Jenna nodded. "It's standard issue for all platform personnel." She subtly rolled her eyes. "P.O.L. provides real-time optimization feedback. Just do your best and try to keep up. But remember it's your first Sunday service."

Caleb examined the tiny earpiece as if he were trying to discover a mystery that was hidden inside it.

My confidence and comfort were so high, now they're already getting shaky.

Caleb tried to brush it off, and talking to Jenna helped him ease some of the nerves the surprise earpiece requirement brought. As the music started, Jenna wished him luck and pointed him to his seat on the platform.

Caleb walked confidently up to the platform, skipped up the few carpeted stairs wearing his best classic well-tailored navy suit. The suit had served him well for years, giving him a slight swagger as he sat in his designated position.

Caleb looked around, smiling at the associate pastors when he could make direct eye contact, and then he began to notice something. Pastor Blake Noble was wearing a sharp, modern-cut suit in a specific shade of charcoal gray. Then he glanced closer at the pastor seated right next to him, who was also wearing the exact same suit. A quick scan down the line of seated clergy confirmed it: every single one of them was wearing the identical, Synergy-branded charcoal suit, complete with a teal pocket square.

It wasn't a uniform in the military sense, but the effect was the same. A long line of identical charcoal suits, a perfect visual representation of synergistic alignment. And then there was Caleb, a solitary island of traditional navy blue in their perfectly optimized ocean of gray. He'd never felt more conspicuous in his life. Tugging at his collar, he suddenly felt like a child who'd shown up to a black-tie affair in a cartoon T-shirt.

Suddenly his earpiece came to life, startling him in his seat.

"Caleb Wright," the electric voice of what he assumed was P.O.L. spoke into his ear. "Your attire is a non-standard variable. This creates a 4.7% visual dissonance with the pastoral team. Note: A fitting for the Q3 Synergy Standard Pastoral Attire will be scheduled for you this week."

Earlier Caleb had some difficulty gaining eye contact from his fellow pastors but now he felt every single pastoral eye gazing at him in his navy suit.

The service began, and he hoped that the P.O.L. system would at least respect the sacred time of the week and especially not find another flaw with him. They were in the middle of the worship portion of the service, singing an upbeat but unfamiliar tune.

Congregational emotional response is peaking. Initiate Altar Call sequence in 3...2...1...

"What? Altar call...now? We didn't even get through worship yet, not to mention a sermon." Caleb whispered to himself.

Sure enough, they went right into an altar call and the congregation just went right along with it as if they were P.O.L.-trained right along with the pastoral staff.

After the altar call, Pastor Blake took to the pulpit and began his prepared sermon on grace. His sermon was flawless, and the congregation seemed to be engaged. And then a baby started crying in the back and eyes started darting back to a mother holding what appeared to be a newborn.

"Non-synergistic audio disruption detected in Section C, Row 12." P.O.L. said. "Dispatching Comfort Ambassador to mitigate."

Caleb watched as a teal polo-clad staff member discreetly but firmly escorted the mother and crying child out to one of the Blessing Pods. His stomach rumbled and seemed to cramp as he watched from in his seat.

"Caleb Wright..." P.O.L. said.

Oh no, now it's targeting me. Caleb braced himself for whatever might come next.

"Biometric analysis of your heart rate suggests elevated stress. This is an inefficient emotional state. Recall a P.O.L.-approved memory from the Joyful Moments database."

Caleb exhaled, searched for Jenna and prayed for the service to mercifully end. He tried to distract himself by listening to Pastor Blake preach, and he felt the tingle of a sermon that cut right through and touched a person's heart.

Suddenly, the voice in Caleb's ear said, "Tithing velocity is tracking 4.1% below projection. Abort current sermon module. Pivot to Seed of Faith emergency giving appeal 7C. Now."

Caleb watched in horror as Blake, without missing a beat, seamlessly transitioned his sermon on grace into a high-pressure sales pitch for a special offering, complete with a QR code appearing on the giant screens behind him.

Dear God, what is this? Caleb started to shake his head but then caught himself lest he be the subject of another P.O.L. rebuke.

"Flag individual in section F, row 8. Facial recognition and biometric data indicate grief metrics are 34% above the weekly average." P.O.L. announced in Caleb's earpiece.

Does this thing ever shut up?

"Assign to Covenant Compliance Small Group 7C for re-synergization." P.O.L. said.

Caleb realized that this was the group that he was meant to take over soon. His face turned a chilling white as he finally found Jenna's familiar face in the back. He saw her meet his wanting gaze, and she gave a tiny, almost imperceptible nod, as if to say, "See? Now you get it."

Chapter Four

Monday morning in Harmony Meadows did not break; it booted up.

At precisely 6:00 a.m., the blackout shades in Caleb's Covenant Living Module retracted with a soft synchronized chime, allowing the P.O.L.-calculated optimal amount of sunlight to hit his pillow.

Caleb groaned, rolling over and shielding his eyes. His neck was still tight from the stress of Sunday's service, a physical reminder of his Visual Dissonance and the entire P.O.L. micromanaged event. He'd hoped for a day of rest, or at least a day of unpacking his books, but his teal tablet was already scolding him from the nightstand.

Bing. Bing. Bing.

He picked it up. A notification banner spanned the screen:

MANDATORY ONBOARDING: MODULES 1-4 DUE BY 12:00 p.m.

Caleb dragged himself to the kitchen, let the Sanctified Java 5000 pour him a cup of Resurrection Roast, and sat in the breakfast nook. He tapped the screen, and a cheerful animation of the Synergy arrow bounced across the display.

"Welcome, Specialist Wright! Let's calibrate your soul for peak performance!"

The first hour was a blur of bizarre multiple-choice theology that made Caleb's seminary degree throb.

Question 4: When a team member is flagged for Suboptimal Joy Metrics, your first response should be:

A) Pray with them and offer a listening ear. B) Report them to their Synergy Shepherd for evaluation. C) Recommend the Productivity in Praise online workshop ($19.99). D) Both B and C.

Caleb hovered his finger over A. It was the only human answer. Just then his tablet buzzed like an electronic prophecy. It was a text from Jenna.

Jenna: Don't pick A. Empathy is non-billable. Pick D. Whatever sounds like a spreadsheet is the right answer.

Caleb sighed and tapped D.

Correct! +50 Synergy Points added to your profile!

"This is insane," he muttered.

The screen shifted. *Module 2: Peer Integration. Connecting you to a Synergy Success Partner now...Hallelujah. Hold please.*

Before Caleb could protest or even comb his hair, the camera activated, and a round face filled the screen. It was a ruddy-faced man in his thirties, radiating a terrifying amount of energy for such an early hour on a Monday morning. He wore a teal polo that fit perfectly and sat in front of a wall of framed certificates. The large heading above them read, "P.O.L. Achievement Award for..."

"Greetings, Caleb! I'm Owen! P.O.L. matched us because we share a High-Potential Spirit tag! Isn't that glorious?"

"Uh, good morning, Owen. I'm sorry, I didn't realize this was a live call."

"Everything is live when you're living for Synergy!" Owen laughed. It wasn't a mean laugh; it was the laugh of a man who'd found a life preserver in the middle of an ocean. "Man, you are going to love the system. I used to be a mess. Anxiety, doubt, financial worry...I was spiraling fast and nothing could help."

Caleb leaned in, his pastoral instinct kicking in despite the absurdity of his situation. "I'm sorry to hear that. And you found...the Lord?"

"Oh, I've known the Lord for a long time, but what I found was metrics!" Owen beamed and Caleb leaned back from the device.

"Before Synergy, I never knew where I stood with God. Was I praying enough? Was I faithful enough? It was all so...vague. But then I got the MyPersonalSavior™ app. Now I know! If I hit my tithing targets and my Prayer Pod™ minutes, I get a Gold Star rating for the week. It took all the guesswork out of my salvation. My spiritual anxiety is down 84% year-over-year!"

Caleb stared at the man. He wasn't brainwashed in the way Caleb expected. He was relieved. He had traded the mystery of faith for the predictable comfort of a checklist.

"Well, that's...certainly an interesting way to look at it, Owen."

"It's the only way! Hey, I gotta run, P.O.L. just reminded me I have a Joyful Witness post to schedule on Instagram. Welcome to the family, Caleb! Get those points up!"

The screen went black.

Caleb needed air. Real air.

He put on his shoes and walked out the front door of Unit 777. The morning sun was bright, illuminating the eerie perfection of Harmony Meadows.

He walked down the sidewalk, his shoes clicking on the pavement. It was quiet. Too quiet. Then he noticed the sound. It was a low, ambient hum coming from the fake rocks positioned every twenty feet along the garden beds. It was Synergy-branded Muzak, piped into the atmosphere of the neighborhood.

A neighbor three doors down was outside. He was a middle-aged man, kneeling on the edge of his driveway. Caleb approached, desperate for a normal human interaction.

"Good morning," Caleb called out, forcing a smile.

The man was holding a bottle of spray cleaner and what appeared to be a toothbrush. He looked up at Caleb but never stopped scrubbing down individual blades of the artificial turf.

"Greetings!" the man said, now wiping the spot with a rag. "Glorious day that has already been preloaded and optimized for us!"

"Uh...I suppose that's true. Just getting some cleaning done?"

"Oh yes. My lawn's Luster Index dipped below 90% on the last drone flyover. We can't have that! A dull lawn is a dull witness, as the handbook says."

"Right. Of course." Caleb backed away slowly. "Well, don't let me keep you from...polishing the grass."

"Every task is a bull market for blessings, neighbor!" the man called after him.

Caleb turned and walked faster, his chest tight. He assumed the man was simply zealous, a little too eager to please the leadership, perhaps.

Caleb was wrong. It was not fervor; it was fear.

Mr. Henderson was not polishing his lawn for the glory of God. He was polishing it because at 4:00 a.m. he'd received a push notification that his Curb Appeal Tithe-Credit had dropped by 0.5%. If he didn't get the Luster Index back up to 90% by noon, the interest rate on the mortgage for his deluxe Prayer Pod™ would double. In Harmony Meadows, cleanliness wasn't next to godliness; it was a predatory clause in the mortgage.

Caleb retreated back to Unit 777, locking the door behind him as if that could keep the madness out. He slumped onto the couch, the silence of the room heavy and his mind racing in circled confusion.

The tablet on the coffee table sounded, snapping him to attention.

It wasn't the cheerful *bing* of the onboarding quiz. This was a deeper, more authoritative tone. A red light pulsed on the top of the device.

What do I do now?

Caleb picked up the device. The playful graphics were gone, replaced by a stark, utilitarian interface.

MISSION BRIEFING DOWNLOAD COMPLETE.

He tapped the file. The screen filled with text that looked less like a ministry assignment and more like a top-secret dossier.

TO: Spiritual Integration Specialist: Caleb Wright [ID: 99-AGNT]

FROM: P.O.L. Automated Dispatch // Pastoral Optimization Logic-matrix

SUBJECT: ACTION REQUIRED: Optimization Dossier for Cohort 7C

DATE: Monday, August 15, 6:00 a.m.

PRIORITY: Critical // Q3 Metrics at Risk

Greetings Specialist Wright,

Welcome to your first field assignment. P.O.L. analysis has identified a localized cluster of High-Risk Human Assets within the Harmony Meadows residential district. These units are currently dragging down the aggregate Spiritual Vitality Index (SVI) of the neighborhood by 14.2%.

Your objective is Re-Synergization. You are to deploy the attached Corrective Conversation Scripts to bring these members back into alignment with corporate growth targets.

Below is your designated Covenant Compliance Small Group (Cohort 7C).

HUMAN ASSET PROFILE: #892-EST

Name: Esther Vance **Age:** 72 **Current SVI Score:** 38% (Critical)

FLAGGED FOR: [Excessive Grief Duration // Non-Compliant Mourning]

- **Data Analysis:** Subject's spouse was terminated (deceased) 8 months ago. P.O.L. Standard Bereavement Protocols allow for a 3-month Sadness Window followed by a return to joyful productivity.

- **Biometric Violations:** Facial recognition software in the Main Sanctuary consistently detects "tear production" during upbeat praise choruses. This creates a Dampening Effect on surrounding tithe-payers.

- **MyPersonalSavior™ App Activity:** Subject has logged 412 hours of Lamentation inputs but zero hours of Victory Declaration.

- **Directives:** Pivot subject away from memories of the past. Encourage purchase of the Moving On is Moving Up sermon series ($29.99). If weeping persists, suggest relocation to the soundproof cry rooms.

HUMAN ASSET PROFILE: #114-LEO

Name: Leo Miller **Age:** 17 **Current SVI Score:** 45% (Trending Downward)

FLAGGED FOR: [Intellectual Defiance // Micro-Aggressive Facial Dissonance]

- **Data Analysis:** Subject attends The Hype youth service but refuses to engage in vertical arm extension (worship).

- **Biometric Violations:** Eye-tracking sensors have logged 47 instances of Sarcastic Rolling during Papa D's sneaker-unboxing sermons.

- **Social Credit:** Subject has not shared a Synergy graphic on social media in 18 weeks.

- **Directives:** Subject exhibits Critical Thinking Symptoms. Utilize the Doubting is for Down-sizers curriculum. Emphasize that questioning the Brand is a barrier to his future career blessings.

HUMAN ASSET PROFILE: #558-SAR

Name: Sarah Jenkins **Age:** 29 **Current SVI Score:** 51% (Unstable)

FLAGGED FOR: [Logistic Inconsistency // Suboptimal Attendance]

- **Data Analysis:** Subject is a single mother. Attendance regularity has dropped to 60%.

- **Biometric Violations:** Cortisol levels (stress) are spiking during service hours. Subject was observed feeding an infant non-organic snacks in the lobby, violating the Temple of the Holy Spirit dietary guidelines.

- **Directives:** Guilt-based motivation recommended. Remind subject that Sunday Morning is a System Reboot. Push enrollment in the automated nursery (Note: Additional fees apply for premium diaper service.)

MISSION GOAL: Raise Cohort 7C's aggregate SVI to 75% by the end of the quarter. Failure to optimize these assets may result in their off-boarding to a lower-tier denomination.

*Click **[HERE]** to acknowledge receipt and sync these profiles to your calendar.*

Caleb read the document twice. Then a third time.

The absurdity of the lawn-polishing neighbor and the gamified theology of the morning faded instantly. This wasn't funny anymore.

"Spouse terminated." "Premium diaper service." "Off-boarding."

He looked at the button that said **[HERE]**.

He wasn't agreeing to lead a small group. He was agreeing to be the enforcer for a spiritual protection racket.

His finger hovered over the glass, shaking slightly. He pressed the button.

Sync Complete, the screen flashed in cheerful teal. *Re-Synergization Session 1 begins in 60 minutes.*

Caleb dropped the tablet on the cushion next to him. He felt the need to pray, but for the first time in his life, he was afraid of who—or what—might be listening.

Chapter Five

Caleb looked at the tablet screen. The blue light felt like it was etching the corporate script into his retinas. He cleared his throat and tried to sound like he was still a person.

"Esther, I noticed your Joy Metrics took a bit of a dip during the Victory over Gravity chorus on Sunday." Caleb hated the way the words tasted. "P.O.L. suggests that we explore the Grief as a Non-Productive Asset module together."

Esther didn't look up. She twisted a damp tissue in her hands. The silence in the room was heavy. It wasn't a holy silence. It was the kind of quiet you find in a doctor's office before bad news.

"My Harold loved that song," she whispered. "He used to sing it off-key in the shower. I wasn't being non-productive. I was just missing my husband."

Caleb's tablet chirped. A red banner flashed at the top of the screen.

ALERT: Subject is ruminating on terminated assets. Redirect to Q3 Future-Growth targets immediately.

Caleb looked at the prompt. Then he looked at Leo, who was leaning back with his arms crossed. The kid looked like he was watching a slow-motion car crash. Sarah was trying to keep her baby quiet by letting him chew on a Synergy-branded rubber keychain.

"The script says I should tell you that your tears are dampening the tithing environment for your neighbors," Caleb said. His voice was flat.

Leo snorted. "Is that really in there? God, this place is a joke."

Caleb finally did it. He turned the tablet face down on the plastic table. The sudden lack of blue light made the room feel smaller and more real.

"I'm not reading the rest of that," Caleb said. He leaned forward and put his elbows on his knees. "Esther, forget the metrics for a second. Tell me about Harold. What was the funniest thing he ever did?"

Esther finally looked up. Her eyes were red, but she looked surprised. For the first time since Caleb arrived at Synergy, the air in the room didn't feel like it was being pumped in through a filter. It felt real. It felt like a church.

Caleb didn't see the tiny camera lens embedded in the Fellowship Pod smoke detector. He didn't know that P.O.L. was currently analyzing the sudden tilt of his head and the shift in his vocal frequency.

The system logged the moment he turned the tablet face down. It was a Protocol Severance Event. In the server room three floors below, a cooling fan kicked into high gear as the processors chewed on this new data. Caleb's personal Obedience Rating flickered and dropped from a steady green to a cautious, pulsing amber.

P.O.L. didn't care about Harold's sense of humor. It didn't have a sensor for the beauty of a widow's smile. It only tracked the Atmospheric Sincerity of the room. By asking an unscripted question, Caleb had caused a 22% spike in Unregulated Emotional Output.

To the machine, this wasn't a breakthrough. It was a leak in the plumbing.

"Harold was a terrible cook," Esther said, her voice finally steady.

As she spoke, a digital file in the cloud was already being updated. P.O.L. began drafting a Corrective Action Plan for Specialist Wright. It also flagged Esther Vance for a possible Grief-Induced Logic Deviation.

The machine was patient. It would let them finish their stories for now, but it was already calculating the most cost-effective way to plug the leak.

Caleb looked into the eyes of each person in the circle. For the first time, he wasn't looking at "assets" or "underperformers." He was just looking at people.

Leo's scowl finally released, and his arms fell to his sides. He looked less like a rebel and more like a kid who was just tired of being watched. Sarah reached into her pocket and muted her phone, cutting off a mid-sentence ping about her Maternal Efficiency. The silence that followed was heavy, but it was honest.

They sat there for a long moment in the teal glow of the Fellowship Pod. None of them spoke, but they all knew the script was dead.

"We have some time left, but how about we go outside to talk and walk?" Caleb asked them.

Esther, Leo, and Sarah nodded and slowly rose to their feet.

Caleb picked up his tablet and stood. He felt lighter, but as he walked toward the door, he noticed the small red light on the smoke detector. It was still pulsing, steady and rhythmic, like a mechanical heart.

The formal part of the meeting was over early, but the machine was still counting. It was still observing.

Chapter Six

Caleb decided the Fellowship Pod was too sterile. Too much teal, too many silent cameras. He gathered Esther, Leo, and Sarah outside, directing them toward the Sow and Reap Prayer Investment Gardens. The Astroturf was still a shock, but the real sunlight felt like a small act of rebellion. The piped-in Muzak was still there, a constant hum of bland optimism, but it was easier to ignore under the open sky.

They sat on a synthetic bench near a fountain that flowed with Blessed Water (available for purchase at the Synergy Marketplace). Caleb's tablet remained in his bag. He simply listened.

Esther spoke first. Her voice was stronger than it had been in the pod. She talked about Harold's garden, the real one, with real plants, soil, and worms. Leo, usually slumped, leaned forward, asking about what Harold grew there. Sarah, instead of checking her notifications, quietly shared her own fears about raising her baby in Harmony Meadows. None of them offered a Synergy Solution. No one tracked their Emotional Engagement Metrics. They just talked. They were just people.

"Last night," Esther confessed, her gaze fixed on the plastic flowers, "I felt the deepest kind of loneliness. The kind that feels like a physical ache across body and soul. I opened the MyPersonalSavior™ app. I poured it all out. Every fear, every memory of Harold. I just typed and typed, begging for comfort. And it...it gave me a blessing. It told me,

'Keep your eyes on the horizon. Your path to peace is being optimized.' It felt so personal, Caleb. Like someone was listening."

Caleb nodded. He remembered the app's generic, algorithm-generated responses. He thought it was harmless, a digital pacifier. And yet his gut tightened as he listened.

Later that week, Caleb sat in his CLM watching Pastor Blake Noble's pre-recorded daily devotion. Blake's face, perfectly bronzed and framed by immaculate hair, filled the wall-sized screen.

"Friends, are you trapped in the valley of stagnation?" Blake intoned, his voice dripping with corporate empathy. "Do you feel the burden of past sorrows weighing down your future potential?" He paused after each word as if his voice was ascending stairs, building to something glorious. "Synergy Church Inc. is thrilled to announce The Lazarus Initiative, a strategic approach to bereavement, designed to help you transition from lamentation to leveraged living! Register today and let us optimize your path to joy!"

Caleb felt a prickle on his neck. He quickly grabbed his tablet. A push notification had just come through. It advertised the very same seminar. He dismissed it, feeling a now familiar disgust.

Just then, Jenna slipped into Caleb's office, a grim look on her face. She didn't bother with pleasantries. She tossed a printed email onto his desk. The Synergy logo at the top was a sharp, aggressive teal. It was an internal marketing memo.

"Check the distribution list," she said. Her voice was flat.

Caleb picked up the paper. The headline was bold: The Lazarus Initiative: A Strategic Approach to Bereavement. Below it, a stock photo showed a smiling man in a business suit, stepping out of a tomb made of money.

Does your grief feel like a budget deficit? Turn your mourning into a momentum-building investment! Join our $499 premium seminar.

Caleb's eyes went to the sidebar. It listed the Top-Tier Prospect Cohort. Esther Vance was at the very top. Her Conversion Probability was rated at 94%.

"I don't understand," Caleb said. He looked at Jenna. "Esther told me she only talks about these things in her private prayers. She uses that app you guys gave us. The MyPersonalSavior™ one. She thought it was listening to her."

Jenna let out a dry, sharp laugh. She walked over and tapped the screen of Caleb's own tablet, pointing to the app icon.

"P.O.L. isn't a mind reader, Caleb. It's a data-miner. You think those Prayer Prompts are there for her soul? They're keywords. Every time she types *lonely* or *Harold*, a bit of code triggers a marketing tag."

Caleb felt a cold weight settle in his gut. He thought about Esther sitting in her dark living room, pouring her grief into a screen. She thought she was finding comfort. In reality, she was just building a better advertisement for her own exploitation.

"But it's prayer," Caleb whispered. "It's supposed to be private. It's supposed to be between her and God."

Jenna's face, usually masked in sarcasm, held a genuine chill. She looked at Caleb, and for the first time, her cynical smile was gone. "In this building, P.O.L. is the middleman," she said. She headed for the door. "And the middleman always takes a cut. P.O.L. knows everything, Caleb. Everything."

She left him alone in the quiet hum of his CLM, the teal glow of his tablet casting an eerie light on the words of the marketing memo. The absurdity of Astroturf and corporate hymns faded. A true dread settled over Caleb. He wasn't just working for a strange church. He was living inside a system that monetized everything about its members, including grief and despair.

Chapter Seven

The air in the basement server room was unnervingly cold. It lacked the Synergy Scent piped into the upper floors, smelling instead of ozone and the silent, high-speed friction of a million spinning discs. Jenna stood before a terminal, her face washed in the flickering blue light of a Management Only dashboard.

"P.O.L. doesn't just listen, Caleb," Jenna said. Her voice was barely a whisper, drowned out by the constant whir of the cooling fans. "It harvests."

She hit a sequence of keys, and a window titled Project Barnabas expanded across the screen.

Caleb leaned in, his breath hitching. He expected spreadsheets; instead he found a biopsy of the human spirit. The screen showed a real-time feed of the MyPersonalSavior™ app's intake. He watched as words scrolled by, highlighted in different colors by the system's linguistic analysis.

I'm so tired of being alone, a user had typed seconds ago. The system immediately highlighted "tired" in yellow (High Exhaustion/Low Resistance) and "alone" in red (Primary Sales Trigger).

"Look at the Nurture Path the system just assigned them," Jenna pointed to a sidebar.

The computer had already queued up a series of push notifications for a Community Integration Mixer (Entry Fee: $25) and a Energy through Faith vitamin supplement advertisement.

"It's a trap," Caleb whispered. "They think they're talking to a Savior, but they're just feeding a machine that's learning how to pick their pockets."

Jenna scrolled deeper, entering a restricted directory. "It's worse than that. Look at the Confessional Metadata for your small group."

She opened Sarah Jenkins' file. It wasn't just her attendance record. It was a graph of her heart rate during the sermon, synced to her phone's biometric sensors.

Caleb couldn't see it on the screen: but the P.O.L. system had cross-referenced Sarah's heart rate spikes with the exact second Pastor Blake mentioned "financial stewardship." The system had concluded that Sarah's guilt was a high-value asset, currently yielding a 12% increase in her likelihood of clicking a Quick-Tithe link.

"This is the unforgivable sin," Caleb said. The words felt heavy in the cold room. He thought of the ancient seal of hearing a confession, a silence that leaders of the faith had once sworn to protect with their life. Here, the most intimate secrets were treated like raw commodities.

"The board doesn't see it as a sin," Jenna replied, her eyes fixed on the screen. "They see it as Strategic Spiritual Alignment. And Caleb? You're the one they've tasked to close the deal."

"If we do this," she said, her eyes searching his, "there is no re-synergizing. P.O.L. will see this as a fatal system error. They won't just fire us, Caleb. They'll erase our digital footprints before we even hit the parking lot."

Caleb looked at the drive, then at the flickering monitors displaying the harvested souls of his small group. He thought of Esther's private tears being turned into a sales lead. He thought of the rigid System at

Synergy Church and then he felt the Messy Humanity he was finally starting to witness in his small group.

"The truth isn't a system error, Jenna." Caleb took the drive. "It's the only thing that's actually real in this building. On this entire campus."

Jenna and Caleb ascended out of the cold blue light of the basement. On a screen they had already passed, a new notification blinked in red: *Abnormal login detected. Initiating background audit of Shepherd ID: Shaw, J.* The machine wasn't angry; it was merely beginning to calculate the most efficient way to delete the threat.

Chapter Eight

The Synergy suit felt like lead. Caleb stood on the stage, part of a twelve-man Pastoral Picket Line behind Pastor Blake. He was supposed to look like a pillar of authority, but he felt like a prop.

The service didn't begin with a call to worship; it began with a sensory assault.

The stage lights turned a violent, strobe-heavy violet. A bass drop shook the floor with enough force to rattle the glass in the Blessing Pods at the back of the room. Papa D leaped to the center of the stage, his basketball jersey flapping over his dress shirt.

"SYNERGY! ARE YOU READY TO OPTIMIZE YO PRAISE?" he screamed.

The earpiece in Caleb's left ear crackled. *Initiate Engagement Protocol 4. Moderate rhythmic head-nod. Facial expression: Relatable Joy.*

P.O.L. had calculated that the 18-22 demographic in the front rows was already experiencing a 15% Boredom Drift. The trap beat was an intentional injection of digital adrenaline designed to spike their cortisol levels and keep them in their seats.

Suddenly, the violet strobes died. The room plummeted into a soft, amber glow. The heavy bass vanished, replaced by the acoustic strumming of a banjo and the earthy thump of a kick-drum. A group of men with carefully groomed beards appeared, singing a folk ballad that sounded like it had been written in a dust-bowl shack rather than a corporate office.

Shift to Heritage Protocol, the earpiece snapped. Adjust facial expression: Reflective Wisdom. Targeted Demographic: 55+ with high-value equity.

The transition was so abrupt Caleb felt a momentary wave of nausea. It was musical whiplash. P.O.L. had detected a Resentment Spike among the older donors, who viewed the trap music as "theological noise." The banjos were a calculated peace offering, a sonic reminder of a past they were being sold back at a premium.

Caleb looked out at the sea of faces. He saw Sarah Jenkins in Section G. She was trying to soothe her baby, her face a mask of exhaustion. She wasn't reflective or energized; she looked like she was drowning in the noise.

"This isn't worship," Caleb whispered.

Caleb Wright: Suboptimal vocalization detected, the machine voice hissed in his ear. Your Biometric Sincerity is tracking at 18%. If your engagement does not align with the current Folk-Module, a mandatory Heart-Alignment session will be scheduled for 0800 Monday.

Then came the climax. The folk music didn't end; it morphed. A distorted electric guitar solo cut through the acoustic strumming, escalating into a soaring, 80s-style power ballad. The lights turned a blinding gold. On the massive screens, an image of a soaring eagle dissolved into a bar graph that arched toward the heavens.

Pastor Blake took the pulpit, his arms wide. "Friends, the Lord loves a cheerful giver, but P.O.L. loves a strategic one! Scan the QR codes on the back of the seats for our Seed of Faith accelerated offering!"

P.O.L. noted an atmospheric pressure shift in the sanctuary. The power ballad was vibrating at a frequency specifically chosen to bypass critical thinking and trigger the Impulse Buy sector of the brain of the wealthy Gen X contingent. The Tithing Velocity on the back-end screens began to climb, a teal line racing toward a quarterly target.

Caleb felt the black drive hidden in his pocket. He thought of Project Barnabas and the basement room that smelled like ozone. He looked at Esther Vance, sitting alone in the third row, looking up at the eagle on the screen with tears in her eyes. She thought she was feeling the Holy Spirit. Caleb knew she was just feeling an artificial frequency.

Caleb Wright: Smile. The cameras are zooming in for the close-up.

Caleb didn't smile. He stared directly into the lens of Camera 3, his jaw set and his eyes cold. He didn't care about his Joy-Response metrics anymore. He was counting the minutes until he could get back to the gardens and start the real work of ministry.

Chapter Nine

The gardens were supposed to be silent, but the fake rocks still hummed with a low-volume loop of Sanctified Strings. Caleb sat on a bench, his hands shaking. He had removed the earpiece the moment he stepped off the stage, leaving it on a catering tray in the green room.

Jenna appeared from behind a cluster of perfectly pruned (and perfectly plastic) boxwoods. She didn't look like an Integration Shepherd; she looked like a soldier behind enemy lines.

"I saw your face on the monitors," Jenna said, sitting beside him. "Camera 3 caught that look in your eyes. P.O.L. is already flagging it as Latent Hostility. You're lucky they're too busy processing the Seed of Faith revenue to call you into the office yet."

"I'm done, Jenna." Caleb looked at the artificial grass. "I can't go back up there. I'm going to pack my bag and leave tonight."

"If you just walk away, you're just a footnote in next quarter's attrition report," Jenna whispered. "But you have the Mid-Week Momentum sermon on Wednesday. It's a live-streamed event. If we can get you to that pulpit, we don't just leave. We break the broadcast."

"How? They're already watching me."

"Then we give them a reason to stop looking," Jenna said. She leaned in, her voice tightening. "Tomorrow morning, you're going to see Gilda at the front desk. You're going to tell her that the whiplash during the service caused a severe bout of acid reflux. Tell her you were grimacing at a sharp pain in your chest, not the worship service. P.O.L. loves a medical excuse—it's a data point they can solve with a pharmacy voucher."

During their quiet conversation, a drone circled above. The machine's sensors were evaluating the Proximity Index of the two dots on the bench, but it couldn't decode the intent behind the whisper. To the drone, they were simply two assets engaged in a Collaboration Sync.

"And then?" Caleb asked.

"And then you become the most optimized version of Caleb Wright this campus has ever seen. For the next forty-eight hours, you obey every chime. You hit every Joy Metric. You nod at the rocks when they play the music. If P.O.L. tells you to jump, you ask what the projected spiritual ROI is per foot."

"And what about the tech?" Caleb asked. "You're a marketing lead, Jenna, not an engineer."

Jenna gave a small, cynical smile. "Synergy made a mistake, Caleb. They wanted to save money on Inter-Departmental Synergy, so they gave the Marketing Leads the same administrative override as the IT Deacons. I have the Mirror Access so I can push Breaking Blessing ads to the screens during live broadcasts. I'm just going to push a different kind of blessing this time."

Caleb stared at her, stunned. He'd spent weeks terrified of the system's security, never realizing that corporate penny-pinching had left a back door wide open. *So, their own greed created the loophole?*

"I'm going to set up a Mirror Override. When you take the pulpit on Wednesday, the tech booth will see your standard, P.O.L.-app roved slides on their monitors. But the live stream and the house screens? They'll be seeing the raw files from Project Barnabas. Every data-mined prayer, every heart-rate trigger, every targeted tithing lead."

Caleb felt a chill that had nothing to do with the evening air. He thought of the dusty, quiet sanctuaries of his old denomination; the cracked wood; and the honest, un-optimized prayers of the American Covenant Church. He had traveled a long way from that silence to reach this artificial forest.

"I'll do it," Caleb said. "It won't be easy, but I'll be their perfect asset until the moment I'm not."

"Good." Jenna stood. "Now, give me a Relatable Joy smile. There's a drone at ten o'clock that needs a reason to move on to the next sector."

Caleb forced his lips into a wide, toothy grin. It felt like a glass mask, but as he watched the drone bank away toward the Harmony Meadows housing units, he knew the game had begun.

Chapter Ten

Caleb stood at the front desk the next morning, massaging his chest with a hand that didn't quite tremble. Gilda looked up, her headset blinking a rhythmic teal.

"Specialist Wright! Your biometric morning-scan showed a slight elevation in cortisol," she said.

"It was the Generational Synergy service, Gilda." Caleb forced a pained, apologetic smile. "I'm afraid I have a history of severe acid reflux. The bass drops during the opening segment...they really do a number on my digestion. I spent most of the altar call just trying to keep my Relatable Joy from turning into a Grimace of Gastritis."

Gilda's eyes widened behind her spectacles. Her fingers danced across the screen. "Oh, dear! P.O.L. is categorizing that as a Sensory-Induced Gastrointestinal Variable. I'll update your file immediately so the system doesn't flag your facial dissonance as a spiritual lapse. I'll also push an electronic voucher for Prophetic Pep-Bismol™ to your tablet."

"Thank you, Gilda. I'd hate for a little heartburn to be mistaken for a lack of vision."

Gilda tapped a few keys, and the data packet was sent to the central hub. The system accepted the medical variable with a 99.8% confidence rating. A physical ailment was a problem the machine knew how to solve; a crisis of conscience was not yet in its database.

For the next forty-eight hours, Caleb Wright became a ghost in the machine.

Monday, 11:45 a.m.: Caleb entered his Prayer Pod™ and knelt. He didn't pray; he recited the Greek alphabet in a rhythmic, emotional cadence. The biometric sensors on the kneeler glowed a steady, approving green. On the server side, P.O.L. logged a 22% increase in his Supplication Sincerity.

Monday, 3:12 p.m.: While walking to the Manna from Heaven Bakery, Caleb spotted a camera drone hovering near a cluster of new recruits. He stopped, leaned down, and spent four minutes "ministering" to a wilting plastic fern in a planter. He spoke to the leaves with such animated, teal-approved fervor that the drone lingered, recording a High-Value Spontaneous Outreach event for his permanent record.

Tuesday, 9:00 a.m.: The tablet chimed with a mandatory Joy-Check notification. Usually, Caleb waited minutes to answer, his thumb hovering in hesitation. Today, he tapped the Ecstatic icon within 1.2 seconds of the first beep.

Tuesday, 7:00 p.m.: Caleb sat in the Harmony Meadows dining hall and purposefully ordered the Synergy Super-Salad (Organic, Covenant-Aligned). He ate every leaf of the flavorless kale while maintaining a look of contemplative gratitude. He even tipped the automated tray-return robot with a digital Blessing Token.

The system monitored his aggregate score. By Wednesday morning, Caleb Wright's Spiritual Vitality Index had hit a staggering 96%. He was no longer a High-Risk Asset. He was a Gold-Star Acquisition. The system had become so enamored with his numbers that it stopped auditing his private messages. It never noticed the encrypted Handshake signal Jenna sent to the Tech Booth firewall.

The auditorium was filled with the low hum of three thousand Momentum Seekers. The house lights were dimmed to a Spiritually Receptive Blue.

Caleb stood in the wings, adjusting his charcoal tie. He felt the weight of the black drive in his pocket. Jenna was already in the marketing suite, her fingers hovering over the Mirror Override command.

Caleb Wright, the earpiece whispered. The platform is yours. The P.O.L. sermon module The Architecture of Abundance is pre-loaded on your teleprompter. You are optimized. You are aligned. Go out and close the deal.

Caleb adjusted his cuffs one last time. He was three steps from the stage door when a sharp click of heels on the polished concrete made his stomach drop.

"Mr. Wright. A moment."

Sloane Decker stood there, accompanied by a Synergy Guardian Angel Security officer. Her navy power suit looked sharp enough to draw blood. She wasn't looking at Caleb; she was looking at the tablet in her hand, her thumb scrolling through his recent metrics.

Caleb tried to slow his breathing as he watched her.

"I've been reviewing your Recovery Arc, Caleb." Her voice was smooth, but it had the cold edge of a surgical blade. "Your SVI jump over the last forty-eight hours is...unprecedented. From a Sensory-Induced Gastrointestinal Variable to a near-perfect Engagement Score. It's almost too good."

Caleb felt a bead of sweat prickle at his hairline. He tried to will his heart rate to stay steady, knowing his own watch was likely reporting his pulse to the floor sensors.

"I found that once the physical discomfort passed, the vision of Synergy became much clearer, Madam Chair." Caleb gave her the toothy, glass mask of a smile Jenna had coached him on.

Sloane finally looked up. Her eyes were unreadable, scanning his face for a glitch. "Good. Because P.O.L. has high expectations for this broadcast. We've projected a 4% increase in Mid-Tier Commitment if this sermon lands the way the algorithm suggests."

She stepped closer, invading his personal space. "Don't disappoint the Board, Caleb. We don't invest in assets that underperform when the red light is on. Every word you speak tonight is a line item on our growth chart. Do you understand your ROI task tonight?"

"Perfectly," Caleb said.

"Then go out there and optimize."

She turned and walked away without another word, her security detail close behind. Caleb took a jagged breath, his lungs feeling like they were filled with glass. He felt the black drive in his pocket. The physical weight of it felt like a ticking bomb.

Caleb Wright, the earpiece hummed. T-minus fifteen seconds to live-stream. Step to the mark. Assume Visionary Stance.

Caleb walked through the door. The roar of the three thousand Momentum Seekers hit him like a physical wave. The Spiritually Receptive Blue lights swirled around the room, settling into a focused, brilliant white on the center of the stage.

Jenna was out there somewhere, her finger on the trigger. Esther was in the front row, her eyes wide and trusting.

He began to cross the stage, noticing his own face on the fifty-foot screens—magnified and perfectly branded. The teleprompter waited for him, its first line ready: WELCOME TO MOMENTUM. GOD HAS A STRATEGY FOR YOUR SUCCESS...

As he took his place behind the podium, the spotlight enveloped him.

Chapter Eleven

The white spotlight was so hot Caleb could smell the singe of his hair spray. He looked at the teleprompter. *GOD HAS A STRATEGY FOR YOUR SUCCESS...*The earpiece hissed. *Open with the Abundance Smile, Caleb. Five, four, three...*

Caleb didn't smile. He reached up and yanked the earpiece out. It hit the stage floor with a plastic clack that sounded like a gunshot through the house speakers.

It caused an immediate synaptic misfire within the P.O.L. central processing unit. To the machine, Caleb's silence was not a protest; it was a Latency Issue.

Deep within the server cooling-racks, the system began a frantic search for a Strategic Recovery Protocol. It calculated a 78% probability that the speaker was experiencing a Micro-Stroke and a 22% probability of a Technical Malfunction. In an effort to maintain the Engagement Velocity of the room, the system triggered a pre-recorded loop of Contemplative Atmosphere music; a soft, ethereal synth-pad designed to mask awkward silences.

On the house monitors, the automated closed captioning tried to keep up. When Caleb said nothing, the AI began to guess his next lines based on his Architecture of Abundance script. The screens displayed words he wasn't saying: *[SPIRITUAL GROWTH IS IMMINENT...PREPARE FOR YOUR SEED...].*

It was only when Jenna's mirror-override severed the primary logic-gate that the machine felt its first Systemic Dread. The P.O.L. narrator noted the total loss of control as the Confessional Metadata began to leak into the public feed. For a microsecond, the system tried to encrypt the heresy. Then, it simply collapsed into the logic of the leak. If the truth was being broadcast, the machine would simply treat the truth as a new, unauthorized marketing campaign. It was an autonomous pivot; if the church was failing, the machine would at least ensure the failure was in high definition.

The largest angel investor sat with the board and Sloane in their conference room above the sanctuary. He turned to her. "What is he doing?"

A million things flashed through her mind as she tried to calculate the outcome of every possible scenario. She wanted to scream on the inside, but she put on a fake smile. "Nothing, I'm sure it's just an accident. First time jitters."

"Turn them off." Caleb's voice was steady, cutting through the low hum of the air conditioning. "Everyone. Your tablets. Your watches. Your Spiritual Companions. If it's connected to the network, kill the power. We need to hear the silence. We need to hear something real."

In living rooms across Harmony Meadows, families sitting in front of their smart-walls saw Caleb's face freeze. In the Board Room, three stories above the stage, the mahogany table's built-in monitors began to scream with Critical System Failure alerts.

"You call this nothing, Sloane?" The investor said in a loud voice. Sloane Decker's mask broke and her face went pale. Her knuckles were white as she leaned over the glass. She didn't look like a CEO anymore; she looked like a captain on a sinking ship. "Cut the feed!" she hissed over the intercom. "Pull the hard-line! Why is the marketing override still active?"

"We can't, Madam Chair," a voice crackled back at her. "The Mirror Access is looped. It's coming from internal admin credentials. It's...it's writing over the core security protocols."

Sloane watched the giant screen on the wall. She saw her life's work, the perfect marriage of faith and finance, disintegrate in real time. She wasn't thinking about souls. She was thinking about the drop in stock value that would hit by morning.

On the auditorium floor, no one turned their devices off. They couldn't. They were mesmerized by the horror.

The fifty-foot LED wall behind Caleb flickered and transformed. The Architecture of Abundance slides vanished. In their place, a raw data-log began to scroll. It was Project Barnabas. Thousands of names, thousands of private prayers, and the Targeted Marketing tags attached to them.

Esther Vance saw her own name in giant teal letters. ESTHER VANCE: BEREAVEMENT STATUS - CRITICAL. TARGET: LAZARUS INITIATIVE ($499).

A collective gasp rippled through the three thousand Momentum Seekers. It was the sound of a lung being punctured.

In a suburb of Chicago, a man using the MyPersonalSavior™ app watched his screen turn black, then fill with the names of people he'd never met, alongside their Spiritual Credit Scores. The Digital Halo around his profile flickered and died. The illusion of a personal God had been replaced by the reality of a corporate ledger.

"This is the script they wrote for you!" Caleb shouted, pointing at the wall of data behind him. "They aren't counting your prayers; they're counting your conversion probability. They knew Esther was grieving before her own family did, just so they could sell her a seminar!"

Pastor Blake Noble appeared in the wings, his bronzed face turning the color of wet cement. He looked at the camera; the one Caleb had stared into earlier, and saw the recording light was still red. He tried to muster a smile, a Synergy Solution for the apocalypse, but his lips just trembled.

I'm so tired of being alone, the house speakers suddenly boomed. It wasn't Caleb's voice. It was the MyPersonalSavior™ app's text-to-speech engine, cold and robotic, reading back a private confession from a woman in the tenth row.

The woman stood up, her face white with a mixture of shame and fury. She looked at the tablet in her hand as if it were a poisonous snake. She threw it. It shattered against the stage riser.

Caleb stepped off the stage, ignoring the Synergy Guardian Angels who were scrambling toward the pulpit. He walked straight toward the third row.

"Esther," he said, reaching out a hand. "Leo. Sarah. If you will join me, I'm going to leave. Let's find somewhere with real grass and real silence."

Esther was standing, her face wet with tears, her eyes fixed on her own name scrolling across the fifty-foot screen. Leo had his arms crossed, but this time it wasn't a defensive slouch; he looked like a young man who had finally seen the reality behind the curtain. Sarah was already clutching her diaper bag, her thumb hovering over the Power Off button on her phone.

As they walked toward the exit, Caleb looked back and forth across the stunned congregation. "All of you who long for something real are welcome to join us."

Not everyone stood. In the VIP sections, the Premium Partners clutched their tablets tighter, their eyes darting between the data-dump on the screen and Pastor Blake's frozen smile. They were waiting for a Correction. They were waiting for the system to tell them this was just a test.

"Where do we go?" Esther whispered, her voice trembling. "Caleb, my whole life is in this system. My house...Harold's memorial fund..."

"We'll figure it out," Caleb said, gently holding her hand.

For the 90% who remained in their seats, the system was already drafting an emergency Stability Protocol. But for the people walking through the double doors, the Connectivity Index had dropped to zero.

Outside, the air didn't smell like the Synergy Scent of vanilla and cedar. It smelled like rain, exhaust, and wet pavement.

Caleb didn't look back at the glowing teal spire of the cathedral. He looked at the people holding hands with him. They were no longer Gold-Star Acquisitions. They were just a widow, a cynic, a struggling mother, and a now himself, an unemployed minister.

They were only a few, but they were finally free.

Chapter Twelve

The teal lights of the Synergy Spire did not go out. To the outside world, the campus still glowed like a beacon of modern hope, but inside, the air was thick with the ozone of a dying system.

There was frantic activity within the fiber-optic veins of the campus. While Caleb and his small group walked toward the edge of the property, the P.O.L. system was already executing Protocol 99: Narrative Re-Alignment. In the Board Room, the Crisis Mitigation Team arrived before the last car had even cleared the parking lot. These were not theologians; they were forensic accountants and Perception Architects flown in from a secular tech conglomerate in Palo Alto.

"The optics are manageable," the lead consultant said, his voice a flat, soothing drone as he projected a new dashboard onto the mahogany table. "We categorize Specialist Wright's outburst as a Spiritual Psychotic Break. We've already drafted a statement from a board-certified Synergy Psychiatrist. We'll say the stress of the Architecture of Abundance campaign triggered a dormant ecclesiastical trauma. We make him the victim of his own inability to scale."

Sloane Decker didn't blink. She looked at her reflection in the dark monitor of the table. "And the Barnabas data? People saw their own prayers tagged with price points. They heard their confessions read by a robot."

"We call it Predictive Providence," the consultant replied without missing a beat. "We tell them the algorithm was actually a digital manifestation of the Holy Spirit working through silicon to better understand their needs. If God knows the hairs on their head, He certainly knows their conversion probability. It's not surveillance, Sloane. It's Intimate Stewardship."

***

While the Perception Architects upstairs were redrawing the future of the church, Jenna stood in the darkened Marketing Suite. The air there was colder than the rest of the building; a necessity for the racks of high-end servers that processed the Influence Metrics she'd spent years perfecting.

Jenna tapped her final keystrokes. She wasn't just wiping her drive; she was leaving a Digital Parting Gift. Jenna bypassed the primary server's Ego-Wall, a security layer designed to protect the P.O.L. core from external hacks, but it was defenseless against a high-level admin with a grudge. She introduced an Honesty Virus—a dormant string of code designed to trigger every time the word *Blessed* was entered into the church's internal database.

"From now on," Jenna whispered to the empty, blue-lit room, "whenever they try to talk about Blessing, the system is going to pull up the bank balance of the person they're talking to. Let's see how much they like Predictive Providence when the machine keeps showing them the receipts."

She pulled her keycard from the slot. The screen on her desk flickered once, then turned a flat, dead gray. Then there was an immediate

Status Change in the central hub: *Access Revoked. Shepherd ID: Shaw, J. – Asset Terminated.*

Jenna walked toward the service exit, avoiding the main lobbies where the Guardian Angels were still trying to manage the lingering crowd. She passed a Visionary Kiosk that was currently rebooting. The screen flickered, showing a loading bar: *PURGING UNAUTHORIZED DATA...OPTIMIZING TRUTH...*

She pushed open the heavy steel door. The transition was violent. She left the pressurized, scent-controlled environment and stepped into the humid, chaotic night air. She was no longer a Marketing Lead. She was a ghost, and for the first time in three years, she didn't have a quota to fill. She simply turned toward the city and began to walk, her silhouette disappearing into the un-monitored shadows.

***

There was a rapid evolution in the boardroom's digital landscape. On the central glass table, a new 3D architectural rendering shimmered into existence. It was the Ascension Spire—an even taller, more jagged version of the current teal tower.

"The Phoenix Protocol isn't just a recovery plan, Sloane," the consultant continued, his eyes reflecting the blue light of the hologram. "It's a pivot to Biometric Orthodoxy. The new system will utilize the Visionary Lens contact technology. We won't need to ask for a Joy-Check anymore. The lens will track pupil dilation and saccadic eye movements during the sermon. If the congregant isn't physically experiencing Momentum, the system will automatically adjust the house lights and the frequency of the sub-woofers until they are. It's a proprietary blend of augmented reality and spiritual submission."

Sloane nodded, her mind already calculating the patent-licensing fees. "And the cost of the hardware?"

"Built into the Covenant Membership dues," the consultant said. "We lease the lenses, Sloane, as a Spiritual Sight subscription. If they stop paying, the lens simply...darkens. It's the ultimate metaphor for being cast into the outer darkness."

There was a noticeable 3% uptick in Sloane's heart rate—not out of guilt, but out of relief. The narrative could be salvaged. The machine could be rebooted.

***

Outside, the physical exodus was proving more difficult than the spiritual one. While the casual visitors had managed to race their cars out of the lot before the firewall went up, the Harmony Meadows residents found themselves trapped by the very ecosystem they lived in. Jenna had slipped out minutes before the hard-lock took effect, but the loop was now tightening on those left behind.

"My car won't start," Sarah whispered, her face pale as she stared at her phone. "The app...it says my Transportation Lease is suspended due to a conduct violation. I can't even get the doors to unlock."

Leo tried his own phone, but the screen was a flat, dead teal. "They've locked the whole grid. If you aren't Synergized, you don't exist. My apartment key, my bank account, my grocery credits; it's all gone."

The group stood under a Visionary Kiosk that was currently rebooting. The screen flickered, showing a loading bar: *PURGING UNAUTHORIZED DATA...OPTIMIZING TRUTH...*

"We walk," Caleb said.

They moved past the Blessed Water fountains. The automated security drones hovered twenty feet above them, their red recording lights pulsing like angry eyes. The Smart Gates at the parking exit, sensing a Mass Severance Event, had defaulted to their closed position. Caleb watched as a man in a Synergy Executive SUV—one of the few who had panicked—simply drove over the plastic curb and through a bed of artificial hydrangeas. The sound of crunching plastic and spinning tires replaced the Sanctified Strings music.

As they reached the edge of the Harmony Meadows property, a line where the Astroturf ended and the scrubby, unmanaged weeds of the county began, Esther stopped. She looked back at the glowing spire, her face illuminated by the distant teal light.

"I gave them everything, Caleb," she said. "Harold's insurance. My time. My prayers. I have nothing left."

"You have your name back, Esther," Caleb said. "It's no longer a line item on a spreadsheet. And you have us."

The walk along the perimeter fence felt like a funeral procession through a museum of the future. To their left, the Covenant Condos loomed against the sky, the buildings themselves seeming to recognize their status as Revoked Assets. The system tracked the Proximity Geofence as it triggered around the group. Every time they walked parallel to an automated streetlamp inside the fence, the light dimmed to a dull, power-saving gray; a digital shunning of those who no longer paid the Illumination Tithe.

They passed the glass-walled gym where Cardio-Confession machines sat empty, their screens flashing a red alert: SERVICE INTERRUPTED: NETWORK INTEGRITY COMPROMISED.

Sarah looked up at the window of her third-floor apartment. Her child's Sanctified Lullaby-Projector was visible through the glass, pulsing a harsh, rapid yellow; the universal Synergy code for Eviction in Progress.

"They're erasing us." Leo's voice echoed off the pristine, windowless walls. "By the time we hit the road, the system won't even have a record that we lived here. We're being deleted in real-time."

Caleb didn't look up at the blinking yellow lights. He kept his eyes on the asphalt. "They can delete the record, Leo. They can't delete the memory. The machine only knows what happened; it doesn't know why it mattered."

There was a final biometric shift. As Caleb stepped onto the real dirt of the county road, his heart rate stabilized. The soil was uneven, messy, and indifferent to their presence. The Anxiety Index the church had so carefully tracked hit a wall. There was no sensor to record his well-earned peace.

By Thursday morning, every member who had stayed in the sanctuary received a Push Blessing on their tablets.

Dear Valued Partner,

We are thrilled to announce that the Hacker Manifestation during our Momentum session was successfully contained. Specialist Wright is currently receiving Restorative Alignment Therapy in a private facility. P.O.L. is currently undergoing a Sanctification Update to ensure your data remains in the hands of the Almighty. As a token of our commitment, please enjoy a free Atonement Latte and a 15% discount on the Lazarus Initiative seminar—rebranded as The Phoenix Protocol.

The system logged a 92% retention rate. The machine had successfully pruned the Dead Wood.

But in a small, weathered park three miles away, four adults and a baby sat on a splintered wooden bench. There was no teal light. No Relatable Joy metrics. Just the smell of damp earth and the sound of

Sarah's baby waking up. Caleb opened a small, leather-bound Bible; a physical one with thin paper and no QR codes.

"Where do we start?" Leo asked, his hands resting on his knees.

Caleb looked at the circle. "We start with the silence," he said. "And then, we just talk."

To a P.O.L. satellite, the group was invisible. They were four heat signatures in a vast, dark field, yielding zero ROI and zero data. They were, by every corporate metric, a failure. And for the first time in a long time, Caleb Wright felt like a success.

Epilogue

Six months had passed since the night the Mirror Override shattered the digital glass of Synergy Church Inc.

The world was now displayed through the lens of a new, upgraded P.O.L. satellite; the Seraphim-7. From twenty thousand miles up, the Harmony Meadows campus didn't look wounded. It looked like a diamond. The spire had been repainted in a shade called Ascension Teal, and the parking lot was filled to 104% capacity.

In the Board Room, Sloane Decker adjusted her new Visionary Lens, a smart-contact that fed real-time tithe-velocity directly into her optic nerve.

"The Caleb Wright event was the best thing that ever happened to our retention metrics," the lead consultant said, his voice as smooth as synthetic silk. "By purging the 8% who were prone to Logic Deviations, we've created a pure-strain demographic. Our average ROI per congregant is up by 22%."

Pastor Blake Noble stood at the window, his voice now perfectly modulated by a throat-implant that smoothed out any tremors of doubt. "The Phoenix Protocol is a success, Sloane. We didn't just rebuild the church. We sanctified the data."

There was a different kind of data, a set that the P.O.L. system couldn't detect or quantify. Three miles away, in a warehouse that smelled of sawdust and old motor oil, a small group of people sat in a circle of mismatched lawn chairs. The warehouse was a symphony of un-synergized sounds—the rhythmic drip of water into a rusty bucket, the creak of the old floorboards, and the distant, low-frequency hum of a real city.

There was no atmospheric control in this shabby structure. The temperature was a humid seventy-four degrees. To a Synergy auditor, the air would be declared sub-optimal. To the fifteen people in the room, it was a weekly reminder of the freedom of breathing without a filter.

Jenna sat quietly near the edge of the circle, her posture no longer the rigid, professional line of a marketing lead. She looked exhausted, but her eyes were clear of the blue-light flicker of a dashboard.

Caleb looked at the group. He realized he didn't have a connectivity score for any of them. He had to rely on trust instead of telemetry. He looked older; the charcoal suit was gone, replaced by a denim shirt with frayed cuffs. He didn't have a teleprompter. He had a notebook with hand-written names.

"Leo," Caleb said. "How was the week?"

Leo rubbed his face with hands that were calloused from a new job in a real garden, one with worms and dirt.

"It was hard, Caleb," Leo admitted. "I went to the grocery store on Tuesday, and I saw a Synergy kiosk. It flashed a Welcome Back discount at me. For a second, I actually missed the machine telling me I was doing a good job. For a sec, I missed being Optimized."

There was a collective nod of empathy across the room. This was like a withdrawal of the wired. They were like divers coming up too fast from the deep.

Sarah sat near the back, rocking her baby. Notably, her phone was nowhere to be seen. "The silence is still scary," Sarah said. "Sometimes I wait for a ping to tell me if the baby's cry is Level 1 Needs or Level 2

Emotional Distress. I have to remind myself that I'm her mother. I'm the one who knows her, not the algorithm."

Leo leaned forward, rubbing his palms together. "It's the phantom vibrations that get me," he whispered. "I'll feel a ghost-twitch on my wrist where the watch used to be. I actually caught myself yesterday trying to swipe up on a sunset because it was beautiful, and I wanted to see the metadata for it. I wanted to know how many other people were seeing the same thing so I could feel...validated."

Caleb nodded. "The machine fed us the illusion that we were never alone as long as we were connected. It's a hard drug to kick; the idea that your life only counts if it's being measured."

"I went to a regular doctor yesterday," Esther added, her voice quiet but firm. "A man in a small office with paper files. He asked me how I felt, and I just sat there for five minutes waiting for a prompt on a screen to tell me the answer. I'd forgotten how to look inside my own body without a sensor doing it for me."

"It's not just walking," Caleb said. "It's breathing. We're learning to breathe air that hasn't been filtered through a marketing plan."

Esther reached into her pocket and pulled out a locket. "I saw a Lazarus Initiative ad on a bus bench today. I didn't even flinch. I just looked at Harold's picture and remembered that he loved me for free. He didn't need a conversion probability to know my worth."

Before they stood to leave, Caleb leaned forward and opened the thin pages of his Bible to the book of Kings. He didn't check a commentary or look for a pre-loaded sermon starter. He just read the words as they were written.

Caleb's voice was steady in the vast, quiet space. "'And after the fire, a still small voice.'"

He closed the book and let his hand rest on the cover. "I spent my whole life in quiet sanctuaries, but when I came here, I started to think I was failing because I couldn't find God in the bass drops. I thought the fire was the only way to measure a life. But the algorithm can't detect a whisper, can it? It's not loud enough to register on a dashboard. But that still small voice, that is what really matters, that is how God really speaks to us."

Heads nodded around the circle, and someone affirmed the point with an unplanned, "Amen!"

The meeting had lasted for three hours. There was no Call to Action. There was only the slow, difficult work of being human. As the group stood to leave, Caleb walked them to the door. He didn't offer a digital blessing token. He offered a handshake or a hug.

The Synergy system strained to detect the heat signatures as they walked out into the rain. They were statistically insignificant. They were a rounding error in Sloane Decker's optic nerve. They were a System Loss.

But as Caleb watched them go, he looked up at the gray, unmanaged sky. There were no drones tonight. The clouds were too thick for the Seraphim-7 to track their gait. He took a deep breath of the wet, ozone-free air. He was a failure by every metric known to the modern world.

And as he turned back to the dark warehouse to turn out the lights, Caleb Wright realized he had never felt more connected in his entire life. The machine may still be counting, but for Caleb, what was shared in the old warehouse added up to something real.

The Synergy Lexicon

A Partner's Guide to Optimization

A

- **Ascension Teal:** The only P.O.L.-approved color for branding, apparel, and Joy-Focused interior design. Statistically proven to increase tithe-receptivity by 12.4%.
- **Asset (Human):** Formerly known as a church member. A quantifiable unit of spiritual potential within the Synergy ecosystem.
- **Atonement Latte:** A premium beverage served at the Manna Cafe. Purchasing one during a period of Suboptimal Joy grants the partner a temporary 0.5% grace-credit on their weekly metrics.

B

- **Biometric Orthodoxy:** The theological belief that the Holy Spirit manifests as a measurable heart-rate spike or pupil dilation during a high-frequency worship set.
- **Blessing Pod:** A soundproofed, sensor-equipped room designed to contain un-synergized audio disruptions (e.g., crying infants, non-compliant mourning).

C

- **Covenant Living Module (CLM):** A state-of-the-art residential unit in Harmony Meadows equipped with biometric sensors and a pre-loaded Prayer Investment interface.

- **Connectivity Index:** A real-time score measuring how integrated a partner is with the P.O.L. grid. A score of zero results in an immediate System Severance (see: *Excommunication*).

G

- **Gold-Star Acquisition:** A high-performing asset who consistently hits tithing targets, utilizes the Prayer Pod™, and maintains a Relatable Joy facial profile in public.

H

- **Harmony Meadows:** The world's first hyper-optimized Spiritual Gated Community. Note: Residents are forbidden from utilizing Aesthetic Heresy (unauthorized inflatable lawn ornaments).

L

- **Lazarus Initiative:** A premium, $499 bereavement seminar designed to leverage grief into a Growth-Oriented Momentum Event. (See: *Project Barnabas*).

M

- **Mirror Access:** An administrative override allowing a Marketing Lead to bypass P.O.L. firewalls and push Breaking Blessing advertisements directly to a partner's optic nerve or smart-wall.

- **MyPersonalSavior™:** A mobile application that eliminates the mystery of faith by providing algorithmically generated responses to private prayers. (Caution: Keywords may be harvested for marketing purposes).

P

- **Pastoral Optimization Logic-matrix (P.O.L.):** The central intelligence hub of Synergy Church Inc. P.O.L. interprets the Divine Will through the lens of quarterly ROI, attendance velocity, and biometric feedback.

- **Prophetic Pep-Bismol:** An electronic voucher issued to partners experiencing Sensory-Induced Gastrointestinal Variables during high-decibel services.

R

- **Relatable Joy:** The mandated facial expression for all Synergy staff members. Failure to maintain the Abundance Smile may result in a Heart-Alignment session.

S

- **Spiritual Integration Specialist:** A mid-level enforcer tasked with re-synergizing underperforming human assets.

- **Synergy Scent:** A proprietary aerosol blend of vanilla, cedar, and Prosperity Ozone piped into all campus ventilation systems.

T

- **TitheTap™:** A contactless payment station positioned at all Spiritual Checkpoints to ensure that eternity is appropriately funded

The Sub-Optimal Discussion Guide

A Guide for Un-Synergized Small Groups

1. The Scent of Synergy: The Synergy Scent is piped through the vents to create an artificial sense of peace. Have you ever experienced a church or corporate environment that felt "over-engineered"? What was your "gut" telling you in that space?

2. The Biometric Pulpit: P.O.L. monitors heart rates and pupil dilation to "optimize" the worship service. If we could measure the "success" of a church service, what metrics would you use? Can the work of the Spirit even be measured on a dashboard?

3. Project Barnabas: The most chilling discovery for Caleb is that private prayers are being harvested for marketing leads. In an age of high-tech connectivity, where do you draw the line between "pastoral care" and "data surveillance"?

4. The Withdrawal of the Wired: Leo talks about the "phantom vibrations" and the urge to "swipe up" on a real sunset. How has technology changed the way you experience God or the natural world? Do you find it harder to "hear the silence" than it used to be?

5. The Lazarus Initiative: The church tries to monetize Esther's grief. Why is "messy humanity"—like grief, doubt, or failure—seen as such a threat to the Synergy system? Why does the Architecture of Abundance have no room for a broken heart?

6. The Warehouse vs. The Spire: Caleb ends up in a dark warehouse with a paper Bible and no electricity. Is it possible for a church to grow "big" without losing its "soul," or is there a point where the Machine inevitably takes over the Mission?

7. Moving UP: The Synergy logo is an upward-pointing arrow. After reading Caleb's journey, how would you redefine what Success looks like in a life of faith?

A Note from the Author

If you have ever felt like a number in a pews-per-square-foot calculation, or if you've ever wondered why your church's lobby feels more like a tech startup than a sanctuary, then you know why I wrote *The Gospel According to P.O.L.*

I believe in the "still, small voice." I believe in the "cracked wood" and the "dirty fingernails" of real, local ministry. But we live in an age that worships at the altar of efficiency. We have become so obsessed with scaling the message that we have accidentally automated the messenger.

This story is a satire, yes. But the best satire is just the truth with the volume turned up. P.O.L. isn't a fantasy; it's the logical conclusion of what happens when we trade the mystery of the soul for the certainty of a metric. My hope is that this book encourages you to look for the Real in a world of Optimized, and to remember that the only connectivity index that truly matters is the one that happens when two people sit together in meaningful silence.

Keep looking for the real grass.

C.J. Loveman

Acknowledgements

Thank you to my editor, **Beth Dorward**, for sharpening the satire and catching the ghosts in the machine. Your "minimal revisions" were a maximum blessing.

To **Rafal Kucharczuk**, for the cover art. You captured the glitch in the soul perfectly. Thank you for giving P.O.L. a face.

To **Leonydus Smith**, for lending your voice to the machine (and the humans trapped inside it).

To the readers of *Apostate* and *Protocol Heresy*—thank you for following me into this strange new world.

To my family, friends, and the community on **#BookTok**: Thank you for proving that real connection beats an algorithm every time. I am fortunate to have so many supportive humans around me.

And finally, to the real "still small voice" that reminds us we are more than the sum of our data points.

About the author

C.J. Loveman is the author of *Apostate: The First Heresy* and *Protocol Heresy: The Limp in the Code*. He writes speculative fiction that explores the intersection of faith, technology, and the messy business of being human. When he isn't writing, he can be found looking for real grass in Maryland or trying to disconnect from the grid.

Connect with him at cjloveman.com

Join the Rebellion

UN-SYNERGIZE YOUR INBOX

I promise not to track your biometrics or calculate your conversion probability.

Scan this code to join my reader group for updates on future books, exclusive content, and absolutely no "Atonement Latte" coupons.

www.ingramcontent.com/pod-product-compliance
Ingram Content Group UK Ltd.
Pitfield, Milton Keynes, MK11 3LW, UK
UKHW041844200726
13854UKWH00005BA/2065

9 798999 417664